Some words about unicorns:

"Add another one!"
Daisy

"Add two more!"
Gabby

"Try three more!"
Daisy

"Try five more!"
Gabby

"It's working!"
Daisy

"It's really working!"
Gabby

"We have lift off!!!"
Daisy & Gabby

More Daisy adventures!

Kes Gray

DAISY

and the trouble with

UNICORNS

RED FOX

RED FOX

UK | USA | Canada | Ireland | Australia
India | New Zealand | South Africa

Red Fox is part of the Penguin Random House group of companies
whose addresses can be found at global.penguinrandomhouse.com.

www.penguin.co.uk
www.puffin.co.uk
www.ladybird.co.uk

Penguin
Random House
UK

First published 2021

001

Character concept copyright © Kes Gray, 2021
Text copyright © Kes Gray, 2021
Illustration concept copyright © Nick Sharratt, 2021
Interior illustrations copyright © Garry Parsons, 2021
Cover illustrations copyright © Garry Parsons, 2021
Unicorn illustration on pages 255-258 © shutterstock

The moral rights of the author and illustrator have been asserted

Printed in Great Britain by Clays Ltd, Elcograf S.p.A.

The authorized representative in the EEA is Penguin Random House Ireland,
Morrison Chambers,32 Nassau Street, Dublin DO2 YH68

A CIP catalogue record for this book is available from the British Library

ISBN: 978-1-7829-5999-1

All correspondence to
Red Fox, Penguin Random House Children's
One Embassy Gardens, New Union Square
5 Nine Elms Lane, London SW8 5DA

MIX
Paper from
responsible sources
FSC® C018179

Penguin Random House is committed to a
sustainable future for our business, our readers
and our planet. This book is made from Forest
Stewardship Council® certified paper.

To the Booneycorns!

CHAPTER 1

The **trouble with unicorns** is they can get you into trouble. Especially toy unicorns who are secretly real unicorns. If toy unicorns just stayed being toy unicorns instead of turning into real unicorns who can whisper in your ear in actual human language, then Gabby and me would never have got told off by our mums. And I wouldn't have been forced to have a bath in the middle of the day!

Gabby and me never even had a unicorn until a week ago. In fact we had made a secret pact to never ever EVER even get a unicorn! I mean, everyone in our school is OBSESSED with them! It's like a great big giant unicorn wizard has cast a huge magic spell over the whole wide world so that the only thing that children can think about is unicorns! Children in our school have unicorn school bags and unicorn pencil cases and unicorn pens and unicorn pencils. Paula Potts has got a unicorn key ring, Sanjay Lapore has a unicorn drinks bottle, Vicky Carrow has unicorn socks, Craig Alexander has a unicorn lunch

2

box, Barry Morely has got a unicorn calculator cover, Jack Beechwhistle says he's got unicorn underpants but we don't believe him, Lottie and Dottie have got matching unicorn duvet covers (not at school, at home) and even Mr Copford our headmaster has a unicorn-shaped air freshener hanging from the mirror inside his car!

It's like the whole world is turning unicorn!

Which is why for ages and ages and ages me and Gabby have been absolutely totally definitely determined to never EVER EVER EVER EVER have anything to do with unicorns. Or to be unicorn obsessed like everyone else. Because we're individuals.

Trouble is, it was Gabby's birthday a week ago and she invited me to her party.

WHICH ISN'T MY FAULT!

CHAPTER 2

Gabby is really lucky. Her birthday is always in the summer holidays when the sun is shining and we don't have to go to school. Mine isn't. My birthday is always in March when the clouds are clouding and we DO have to go to school. (Unless my birthday's on the weekend. Which it hardly ever is.)

When Gabby phoned me to ask if I would like to come to her birthday party I was really pleased. I knew she was going to ask me because she always invites me to her birthday party. (We're BFFs forever.)

I was even more pleased this time though, because this time she wanted me to be her guest of honour!

The **trouble with being a guest of honour** is you can't just be one. You have to be asked by someone who wants to honour you.

"I've decided to keep things really small," Gabby said, "so we can have each other all to ourselves!"

When I realized that not only was I going to be honoured at Gabby's birthday party but I was going to be the only friend who was actually invited to her party (apart from her mum, dad, nana and grandad, and they don't count because they're family, not friends), I nearly dropped the phone!

"I'd love to be guest of honour at your party!" I said to her, giving the phone a big kiss. "I'd be honoured to be guest of honour at your party!"

Trouble is, then I suddenly had a terrible thought.

"Wait a moment," I said. "If you keep your party really small you won't get any presents! Well, hardly any. You'll only get one from me!"

"I don't care," laughed Gabby. "My mum and dad always buy me loads of presents. And they give me birthday money. Plus my nana and grandad will bring me a present so I won't need any more than that."

"Well, you'll definitely want my present!" I said, already knowing exactly what my present to Gabby was going to be.

"It's not a unicorn, is it?" she laughed.

"Of course it's not a unicorn!" I giggled. "It's much, much better than that!"

As soon as I finished my phone call to Gabby I ran to tell my mum I was going to be guest of honour at Gabby's party.

"You and Gabby are like two peas in a pod," she smiled.

"I prefer conkers in a shell," I said. "You know I don't like peas."

"Well, whatever you're like," said my mum, "you are very lucky to have each other."

"I need to wrap Gabby's present!" I said, jumping up from the sofa and charging up the stairs.

"I've hidden it in the bottom of my wardrobe," shouted my mum. "It's inside my suitcase!"

"I know," I shouted back. "I found it there on Sunday!"

The **trouble with presents** is they need

to be wrapped really properly, especially if the present is a *Sky Pirate All Action Stunt Kite!* Sky Pirate All Action Stunt Kites are one of the best kites you can get.

They're a really exciting shape, they are really good colours, they've got *All Action* strings, plus my mum could actually afford to buy one AND have money left over to buy wrapping paper too! Not just any old wrapping paper either; wrapping paper that had blue sky and seagulls all over it! (Seagulls fly in the sky and so do kites, so a pattern like that is absolutely perfect for wrapping up a kite in!)

"Where is the wrapping paper?" I shouted from the top of the stairs. I absolutely couldn't wait to start wrapping!

"It's under my bed!" shouted my mum.

"Where's the sticky tape?" I shouted.

"Where it always is!" shouted my mum.

"Where are the sharp scissors?" I shouted.

"Out of harm's way!" shouted my mum.

When I had finally got all the things I needed (not including the sharp scissors) I laid everything out on my bedroom floor and got ready to wrap.

Trouble is, everything got a bit complicated after that.

The **trouble with Sky Pirate All Action Stunt Kites** is their really exciting shape makes them really difficult to wrap.

The **trouble with rolls of wrapping paper** is they keep rolling up into rolls again after you have unrolled them. Especially if you let go with both hands.

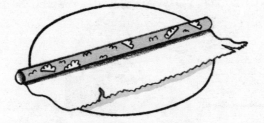

The **trouble with blunt scissors** is they're not in the slightest bit sharp and they won't cut straight either!

And the **trouble with sticky tape** is it sticks to absolutely anything! It sticks to fingers, it sticks to blunt scissors, it sticks to carpet, it sticks to your nose, it sticks to your bed, it even sticks to itself!!!!

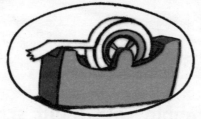

So in the end I got my mum to wrap Gabby's present instead.

I wrote the label though.

Mum stuck it on.

CHAPTER 3

When I woke up on Wednesday I wasn't at all sure what to wear. After all, it's not every day that you are guest of honour at someone's party!

"Have you got any jewels I can borrow?" I asked my mum during breakfast.

"Of course," said my mum. "What would you like? Diamonds, sapphires, rubies or emeralds?"

"REALLY?!" I gasped.

"No, not really, Daisy," she sighed.

"What about a fur coat then?" I asked. "Or something golden?"

"There's a denim jacket in my wardrobe and some golden syrup in the kitchen cupboard," she said.

"How am I meant to look like a guest of honour at Gabby's party if I'm not wearing jewels, a fur coat or anything golden?" I said.

"Just go as yourself, Daisy," my mum smiled. "Gabby has invited her best friend Daisy Butters to her party, not the Right Honourable Miss Daisy Buttersby-Smythe. If you turn up looking like a mayoress she'll probably end up curtseying to you all day."

"What's wrong with that?" I asked.

"It's Gabby's birthday, not yours," said my mum. "That's what's wrong with that!"

"What about something silver?" I asked. "Or silver looking?"

"You can borrow my silver necklace on four conditions," said my mum.

"What conditions?" I asked excitedly.

"One: you don't break it," said my mum.

"I promise I won't break it." I nodded.

"Two: you don't lose it."

"I promise I won't lose it."

"Three: you don't even think of taking it off until you get home from the party."

"I won't even WANT to take it off when I get home from the party!!!" I smiled.

"And four: you put all the breakfast things in the dishwasher."

"Oh, Mummmmm!" I groaned. "I can't load breakfast things into a dishwasher. I'm guest of honour at Gabby's birthday party today!!!!"

"Not until three o'clock this afternoon you're not," said my mum, undoing her silver necklace and dangling it right in front of my eyes. "Bowls, plates, cutlery and cups all in the dishwasher please, Daisy, and you can put the cereal boxes back in the cupboard too, please. And the milk back in the fridge."

Honestly, can you believe it? An actual guest of honour being forced to do things like that?!

Oh well, I guess it was worth it in the end because at twenty to three that afternoon my mum actually did undo her silver necklace again and fastened it around my very own actual neck!

You should have seen me! You should have seen it!! Mum's silver necklace went SO well with my orange T-shirt and purple shorts!!!! Who cares if my trainers were a bit old.

I had Gabby's birthday card in my hand, I had Gabby's birthday present under my arm and I had a necklace of honour hanging around my neck. I had never felt so important in my entire life!

"We could pretend you're my chauffeur, couldn't we!" I said as me and Mum walked down our garden path to the car.

"Don't push it," Mum frowned as she opened the car doors. "And don't play with my rearview mirror," she said as she buckled herself into her seat.

"But I need to see my necklace!" I said, twisting her mirror round and down to face me.

"And I need to be able to see the traffic on the road behind me!" growled Mum, twisting the mirror up and back towards her.

"Don't touch," she said.

"Oh Mum!" I said.

"Let go," she said.

It was a good job it was still only about a ten-minute drive to Gabby's or I think Mum's mirror might have got pulled off! We would definitely have crashed the car. Well, Mum would have.

Normally, my mum would always walk me to Gabby's, especially if it's sunny. Only she had decided to go to **HARDWARE HAVEN** after dropping me off. Apparently, the squeak I've been hearing in our bathroom isn't a mouse singing in the bath: it's the hinges on our bathroom cabinet door.

Mum says the best way to stop squeaky hinges on a bathroom cabinet door is to squirt them with anti-squeak oil. Or buy a new bathroom cabinet. We can't afford a new bathroom cabinet at the moment, though, so if you need to buy anti-squeak oil, **HARDWARE HAVEN** is definitely the place to go.

I don't know where I'd need to go if I wanted to buy a mouse who can sing in the bath. If I did, then I might even have chosen that over a Sky Pirate All Action Stunt Kite!

Except Gabby's got a cat called Satan, who likes eating mice.

So I probably wouldn't.

CHAPTER 4

Did I tell you Gabby has a new house? She moved there at the beginning of the school holidays. It's really new and really posh; it's even got a doorbell that does three different tunes!

When we got there, I could see Gabby already standing on her doorstep waiting for me to arrive. Which was really brilliant but a bit disappointing at the same time, because I wanted to press the doorbell.

Gabby was wearing a blue party hat on her head and a big wide silvery-coloured ribbon over her shoulder that said 'BIRTHDAY GIRL!'.

Mum told me to be on my very best

behaviour and then helped me get the kite from the back of our car.

"Is that for me?" shouted Gabby as we lifted it out.

"You bet!!" I shouted back. "You'll never guess what it is! It's a Sky Pirate All Action Stunt Kite with action grip handles plus action strings and everything!"

That's the **trouble with really exciting birthday presents**. It's impossible not to blab.

Gabby looked really pleased with the present I'd given her even before she'd opened it! Thank goodness I hadn't bought her a mouse that could sing in the bath.

"Bye Mum!" I said, turning around with a wave. "See you at seven!"

Mum drew a circle in the air at me with her finger and then pointed to her neck.

"I won't break it, I promise!" I said, giving her necklace a little wiggle.

Then Mum wagged her finger, put her hands around her own throat and started wobbling her head.

I'm not sure what she meant by that.

"Come and see all my other presents," Gabby said, tugging me into the hallway.

"It's solid actual silver," I said, giving her first look at my necklace before anyone else got a chance to see it. "Because you're my most special friend, my mum said that I could wear it!"

Gabby squeezed my hand really tightly.

"I'm honoured!" she said.

"No, I'm honoured!" I said.

"No, I'm honoured," she smiled.

"No, I'm honoured," I chuckled.

"OK, we're both honoured," she giggled, pulling me through into the lounge.

"Hello Daisy!" said Gabby's mum and dad the moment I stepped into the lounge. They were sitting on the sofa holding cups of tea and wearing party hats too.

"Hello," I said, with a waggle of my necklace. "My mum let me borrow it."

Gabby's mum put her cup of tea down straight away and came right up to my chain for a closer look.

"It's beautiful," she said.

"Look, Daisy's bought me a stunt kite!" said Gabby, tearing off the wrapping paper before I had a chance to say my necklace was solid actual silver.

"How wonderful!" said Gabby's mum, picking the wrapping paper up off the floor and putting it in the bin. "Your dad will enjoy playing with that as much as you will!"

Gabby's mum was right. Gabby's dad is the most outdoorsy grown-up I know. He does camping and walking and stick whittling and everything. In fact he is so outdoorsy he started setting it up straight away so we could play with it in Gabby's new garden!

"Come and see what else I got for my birthday," said Gabby, yanking me out of the lounge and dragging me up the stairs.

"I thought you said your nana and grandad were coming to your party?" I said as she pulled me into her bedroom.

"They are," said Gabby, "but my nana is having her hair done first. She's always having her hair done!"

Gabby's bedroom was absolutely rammed with birthday presents. There were birthday presents on the bed, there were birthday presents on the floor, there was even a birthday balloon dangling from the ceiling!

"I got a Stargazer telescope," she said, "I got a science kit, I got a 3D jigsaw, I got some hair straighteners, I got some juggling balls, I got a bonsai tree growing kit, I got a bath bomb, oh yes, and I got a new bike, but that's in the garage."

"You certainly got a lot of presents!" I said. "Which one is your favourite?"

"YOUR KITE!" she beamed. "Let's go

and see if Dad's finished getting it ready!"

The **trouble with kites** is it really needs to be a windy day to fly one, especially a Sky Pirate All Action Stunt Kite.

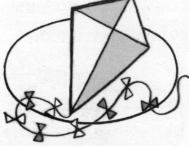

After about five goes we'd only got it to fly as high as Gabby's fence, so in the end we decided to play with Gabby's other presents instead. Well, try to play with them...

The **trouble with Stargazer telescopes** is stars only come out at night, not the middle of the afternoon, especially on really hot days in the summer. So it wasn't really the best time to gaze through a Stargazer telescope, unless we wanted to just gaze at normal sky. Which we didn't.

So we opened Gabby's 3D jigsaw instead.

The **trouble with 3D jigsaws** is they are really hard to do. Especially 1000-piece 3D jigsaws. Gabby's 1000-piece

3D jigsaw was meant to look like the Houses of Parliament but when we took the lid off the box it was just a load of jigsaw pieces in a bag. Which meant we had to make it ourselves! And read the rules on how to make it!!

So we decided to grow some bonsai trees instead.

The **trouble with growing bonsai trees** is before they've actually grown into bonsai trees they just look like seeds. Plus, once you've planted the seeds in their flowerpots they don't even look like seeds. They just look like earth, because that's what the instructions tell you to cover them with.

Gabby said that once we'd watered them the bonsai trees would probably start to grow. But they didn't. Even when we tried watering them with lemonade they didn't grow.

So we tried doing some juggling instead.

The **trouble with juggling** is you really need juggling balls that juggle by themselves, otherwise the balls keep falling on the floor.

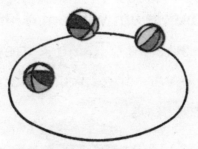

When we looked at the instructions in the juggling ball box, juggling looked really easy, because in the picture the juggling balls were totally still in mid-air. Plus the boy in the picture was really smiling. But the juggling balls didn't stay totally still in mid-air when Gabby and me tried juggling with them. Our juggling balls went all over the place!

So we decided to try out her science kit instead.

The **trouble with science kits** is they are very scientific. In fact they are so scientific even the instructions come with instructions!

"Do you think your mum and dad would show us what to do or will we have to read all of the instructions before we start experimenting?" I asked.

"They're in the kitchen getting everything ready for my birthday tea," said Gabby. "I don't think they'll have time to do experiments at the moment."

"What if we make up our own experiments?" I said.

"We might blow the house up," said Gabby.

"Let's straighten our hair then," I said.

The **trouble with straightening our hair** is our hair was already straight. So that didn't take long to do at all. Even with not-very-hot hair straighteners.

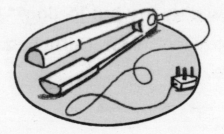

Which only left the bath bomb.

The **trouble with bath bombs** is they are not very exciting unless you are actually in the bath with them.

If you're not in the actual bath with the actual bath bomb you won't be in the water when the water changes colour. Plus you won't be able to feel the bubbles fizzing around your toes.

"How dirty are you feeling?" I asked.

"Not very," said Gabby. "I had a

shower this morning. How about you?"

"Not very," I said, "plus I didn't bring a towel."

"MY BIKE!" said Gabby. "I FORGOT TO SHOW YOU MY NEW BIKE!"

Can you believe it? Out of ALL of Gabby's new birthday presents, she had completely forgotten to show me the biggest and most expensive present she'd been given! What a dipsy brain!

"Race you to the garage!" she said, jumping off the bed and charging down the stairs. "Last one to my garage is a Cheese String!"

CHAPTER 5

"You're a Cheese String!" laughed Gabby, opening the garage doors from *inside* the actual garage.

"You're a cheater!" I frowned, watching the garage doors open from *outside* the actual garage.

"I took a shortcut through the kitchen!" Gabby giggled.

It was true! Gabby was so fast running down the stairs, I didn't see her go through the kitchen!

I thought she'd gone down the hallway and out through the front door.

Imagine having an actual door to your actual garage in your actual kitchen! Not an actual garage door that lifts up or anything but a normal actual kitchen door that gets you into the garage much quicker! I told you Gabby's new house was posh.

"My mum says my nana and grandad will be here really soon," said Gabby. "As soon as they arrive we'll be sitting down for my birthday tea!"

"SHOW ME YOUR BIKE THEN! SHOW ME YOUR BIKE!" I said, ducking under the garage door for a look.

"There it is," she said, pointing to the far wall.

"It looks quite big," I said.

"It is quite big," said Gabby. "My dad chose it. He says we can go forest trekking on it."

"What, like the forest in Potts Wood?" I asked.

"I guess so," she said.

"Where's the basket?" I asked.

"It hasn't got a basket," she said.

"Where's the bell?"

"It hasn't got a bell," she said.

"Where are the tassles on the handlebars?" I asked.

"It doesn't have tassles on the handlebars," she said.

"Why are the tyres so big?" I asked.

"They're mountain bike tyres," she said.

"Why are the metal bits so fat?" I asked.

"That's what mountain bikes have," said Gabby. "Big tyres and fat metal."

"What sort of colour is that?" I asked.

"It's called 'Moss'," she said.

"What do these do?" I asked, pointing to the middle of the back wheel.

"They're the gears," said Gabby.

"What do gears do?" I asked.

"They help you get up mountains," she said.

"Where's the nearest mountain to here?" I asked.

"I don't really know," she said.

"Does it do anything else?" I asked.

"I don't think so," she said.

Gabby's new bike was amazing. If I got a new bike like that for my birthday I would never forget to tell or show anyone. Especially Jack Beechwhistle.

"Can I have a go?" I asked.

"Of course you can," smiled Gabby. "Have as many goes as you like! If you can get on it."

The **trouble with getting on Gabby's new bike** is the saddle came up to my shoulders, plus when I tried to lift my leg over the metal bit my purple shorts started to split.

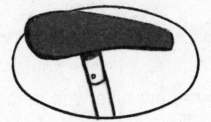

"I'll have a go when I'm a bit older,"
I told her.

"Good idea." Gabby nodded.

CHAPTER 6

Not having a go on Gabby's new bike was a really good idea actually, because just as I was leaning it back against the wall, her nana and grandad turned up in their car.

"They're here!" Gabby squealed, running down the driveway to give her nana and grandad a big hug.

"Daisy, come and meet my nana and grandad!" she said, waving me over to join them.

As soon as I'd got my necklace straight, I went to say hello.

"Daisy, Daisy, Daisy!" said her nana. "We've heard so much about you!"

"Hello," I gulped, forgetting all about my necklace and staring straight at Gabby's nana's hair.

"This is my Nana Pru," said Gabby, "and this is my Grandad Hugh."

"Hello Daisy," said Grandad Hugh. "I hope you haven't eaten all the birthday tea!"

The **trouble with being asked if you've eaten all the birthday tea** is, I couldn't really think what to say back.

Even though I hadn't even seen the birthday tea. Because I was still looking at Gabby's nana's hair. And looking and looking and looking.

Luckily Gabby answered for me.

"Of course we haven't eaten all the birthday tea, you sillies!" she laughed. "We've been waiting for you to arrive first!"

Gabby's nana and grandad took some bags out of their car and then followed our shortcut through the garage back to the kitchen. Which was a bit disappointing again actually, because now I'd missed out on two chances to ring the doorbell.

"I'm worn out!" said Gabby's mum, undoing her apron and wiping her forehead with her arm. No wonder she was worn out! There were empty party food packets everywhere!

"Why has your nana got blue hair?" I whispered to Gabby, while the grown-ups were hugging and kissing.

"She always has blue hair," Gabby whispered back. "She says it stops her looking like a fuddy-duddy."

"What's a fuddy-duddy?" I whispered, as we followed all the grown-ups through to the dining room.

"It's an old person who acts like an old person," Gabby whispered back.

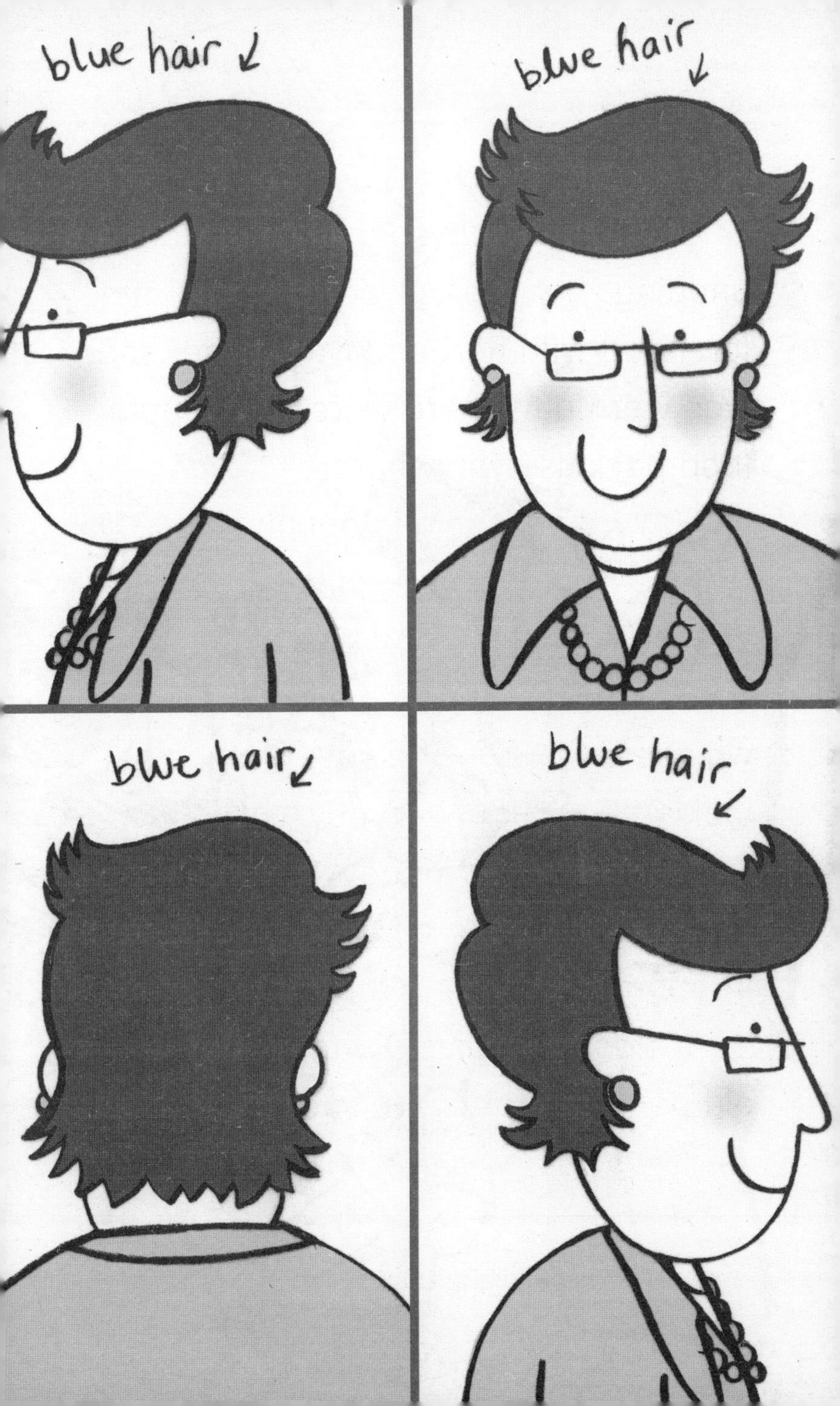

When we got into Gabby's dining room, there was much more than blue hair to look at. There was party food and party cakes and party plates and party poppers and party balloons and party cups and party drinks and pretty much party everything, including a whopping great rainbow birthday cake with hundreds of candles all over it! (Gabby loves blowing out candles!)

"Let the birthday celebrations begin!" said Nana Pru, waving her hands like an octopus and then picking up a blue party napkin. "Hip hip hooray for Gabriella's special day!"

"Pru is short for Prudence," whispered

Gabby, as we sat down at the table. "Just like Gabby is short for Gabriella."

"I've never heard of anybody being called Prudence before," I whispered back. "What's Hugh short for?"

"It isn't!" giggled Gabby, passing me the sausages on sticks.

"How does your nana make her hair go blue?" I whispered.

"Her hairdresser does it for her," whispered Gabby, passing me the mini pork pies.

"Does she have a blue hair brush?" I whispered.

"I don't know," whispered Gabby, passing me the pizza bites. "I've never seen her brush her hair."

"She wears lots of blue jewellery, doesn't she?" I whispered.

"She loves blue jewellery," whispered Gabby, passing me the sausage rolls. "When she dies she's going to give it all to me."

"When is she going to die?" I whispered.

"Not for ages, I reckon," whispered Gabby, topping up my glass with orange squash.

"Why is she wearing two watches?" I whispered.

"In case one of them stops ticking," whispered Gabby, passing me the bowl of crisps.

"Why are some of her fingernails light blue and other ones dark blue?" I whispered.

"They match her hair in different kinds of ways," whispered Gabby, passing me the chicken drumsticks.

Gabby's nana's fingernails didn't just match her hair. They matched her blue dress, her blue shoes, her blue earrings, her blue handbag, her blue necklaces, her blue bracelets, her blue watch straps, her blue eyes and her blue glasses too.

And her blue party serviette.

She was different to any type of nana I'd ever seen before.

She was really good at talking, too.

"Are you having a lovely birthday, Gabriella?" she asked.

"How are you getting on at school, Gabriella?"

"Do you and Daisy sit next to each

other in class, Gabriella?"

"Do you like pop music, Gabriella?"

"Do you like dancing, Gabriella? Your Grandad Hugh and I were wonderful dancers, Gabriella."

"Did you get all the presents you asked for, Gabriella?"

"Grandad and I are going to give you our special present after tea, Gabriella!"

"Have I told you about my childhood, Gabriella?"

It wasn't until it was time to close the curtains and light the candles on Gabby's cake that anyone else really got a chance to say anything much at all. Even then it was only sixteen really loud words...

HAPPY BIRTHDAY TO YOU, HAPPY BIRTHDAY TO YOU, HAPPY BIRTHDAY DEAR GABRIELLA (I said "Gabby") HAPPY BIRTHDAY TO YOU!

As soon as Gabby had blown out her candles, everyone cheered and clapped really loudly. Grandad Hugh even asked Gabby to do a speech! But she was too shy.

Well at first she was, but then she changed her mind.

"Ahem," said Gabby, standing up from her chair and going a bit red. "I'd just like to say thank you for coming to my party and a specially really big thank you to Daisy for being my guest of honour!"

Which meant it was my turn to go a bit red now because then everyone started clapping me as well!

"It's solid actual silver," was the only thing I could think of to say.

"Oh and thank you for my presents!" said Gabby, standing up as soon as she had sat down because she nearly forgot to mention her presents at all!

"PRESENTS!" said Nana Pru, standing up too and waving her hands like ten octopuses this time.

"IT'S PRESSIE TIME, IT'S PRESSIE TIME! YOU'RE GOING TO ABSOLUTELY ADORE THE SPECIAL PRESENTS YOUR GRANDAD HUGH AND I HAVE BOUGHT YOU, GABRIELLA! JUST WAIT TILL YOU SEE WHAT NANA AND GRANDAD HAVE BOUGHT YOU!"

CHAPTER 7

The **trouble with special presents** is sometimes they don't look special at all. Especially if the special present is a toy unicorn.

Double especially if the special present turns out to be (gulp) TWO TOY UNICORNS!

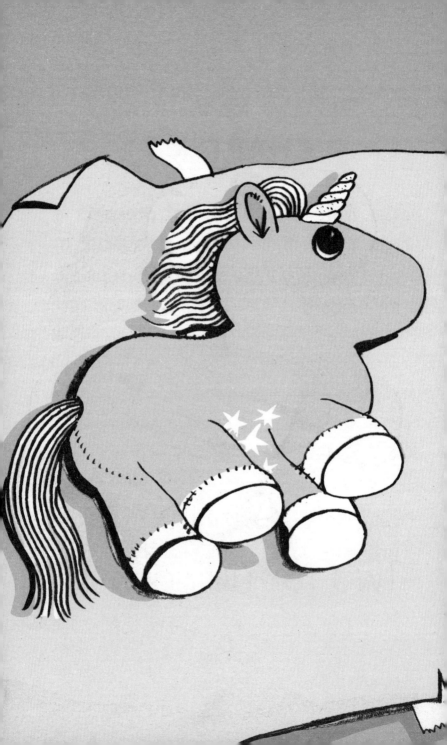

When Gabby unwrapped the paper from her nana's special present I think she had a heart attack. She couldn't move her lips. Or her feet or her arms. Her eyeballs definitely had a heart attack.

"The unicorn with the blue hair can remind you of me, Gabriella!" said Nana Pru. "And the unicorn with the silver hair can remind you of Grandad Hugh! See! Blue hair, silver hair! Aren't they wonderful, Gabriella? Aren't they magical? When I saw them I just had to buy them!"

The **trouble with your eyeballs having a heart attack** is you need your eyeballs to look at someone when they are talking to you. All Gabby could look at was the unicorns.

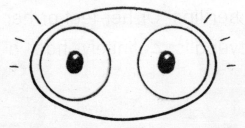

Luckily her lips eventually managed to move.

"Thank you, they're lovely," she said, putting the unicorns on the table right in front of me. "Aren't they, Daisy?!"

As soon as Gabby said "Aren't they Daisy," my eyeballs had a heart attack too. Which meant the more I looked the more my lips wouldn't move either.

Both of the unicorns were really unicorny. The one with blue hair had a white fluffy body and the one with the silver hair had a blue fluffy body. Both of them had glittery horns and long stripy tails.

"Aren't they, Daisy?" said Gabby again, tapping my chair with her toe.

"Yes," I said, finally getting my lips to move. "They're unicorns," I said. "With horns," I said. "Shall we go and play with them in your bedroom?"

How I managed to think of saying the last bit I said I really do not know, but it was a stroke of absolute genius!

Gabby thought so too!!

"Yes, let's!" she said, looking at me with "really well done" eyes!

"Don't you want a piece of birthday cake first?" asked her mum, pulling off the candles, picking up a knife and getting ready to cut the first slice.

"We're a bit full," said Gabby. "Aren't we, Daisy? Do you mind if we have a piece a bit later?"

Gabby's mum didn't mind at all. She just cut four slices for the grown-ups instead.

"Don't forget your wonderful unicorns, Gabriella!" laughed Nana Pru, waving her slice of birthday cake at us as we headed straight for the door.

Gabby and I turned around and gulped. The unicorns were still on the table. It was so embarrassing; far too embarrassing for either of us to think of anything to say at all.

"Remember," said Nana Pru, "I'm the one with the blue hair, Gabriella, and the one with the silver hair is Grandad Hugh!"

Gabby's lips still couldn't think of anything to say, so she just did a sort of laugh instead. More of a snort actually. Then she went back to the table, picked up the unicorns and followed me up the stairs.

As soon as we got into her bedroom we collapsed on to her bed.

"UNICORNS!" she spluttered. "Can you believe it! My nana has bought me unicorns!"

"What are you going to do with them?" I asked.

"Give them to a charity shop," said Gabby.

"What if the charity shop doesn't want them?" I asked.

"Then I'll hide them somewhere," said Gabby.

"Did you like it when I said we should go and play with them upstairs!" I chuckled.

"I loved it!" said Gabby. "I thought we were going to be stuck at the table with two unicorns for the rest of my entire party!"

"We're not going to play with them though, are we?" I frowned.

"Definitely not!" said Gabby, stuffing the unicorns under her bed. "We can play with all my other birthday presents instead."

Except we couldn't. Because we had already tried playing with Gabby's other birthday presents before Nana Pru and Grandad Hugh had arrived.

"We could play with that balloon," I said, lying on my back and peering up at the ceiling. "What's it doing up here in your bedroom?"

"I nabbed it from the dining room!" smiled Gabby. "When Dad was blowing them up."

"Why that one?" I asked.

"It had the longest string," said Gabby, reaching up with her fingers to see how near they could stretch.

"I bet your Nana Pru's fingernails could reach that balloon," I said, having a go myself. "Your nana's fingernails are really long."

"They're not real fingernails," said Gabby. "My mum calls them falsies."

"What are falsies?" I asked, putting a pillow under my shoulders to get me a bit closer to the balloon.

"Fingernails that are false," said Gabby, putting another pillow PLUS ME AND MY PILLOW under her shoulders to see how close she could get.

That's the **trouble with birthday balloons**. Sometimes the strings can be really hard to reach. Especially if you're lying on your back.

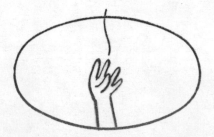

"How do they get balloons to stay up in the air like that?" I gasped, pushing Gabby off my chest so that I could actually breathe. "When I have balloons at home they don't float up into the air. My balloons at home just stay on the floor. Unless I'm playing with them."

"Helium," said Gabby.

"WHATium??" I asked.

"It's like a really light type of air," said Gabby. "My dad has a helium gas canister in the garage. He used it to blow up all of my party balloons."

"Do you reckon if instead of having pizza bites and sausage rolls and chicken drumsticks for your birthday tea we'd had helium instead, we'd all float up to the ceiling too?" I chuckled.

"Probably!" giggled Gabby. "We'd all have to have strings tied to us to stop us floating away!"

"Imagine if the window opened by mistake and we all floated up into the sky!" I said.

"To the moon!" giggled Gabby.

"To the stars!" I chuckled.

"To the universe and beyond!" Gabby grinned.

"I'd love that," sighed Gabby.

"Me too," I smiled. "As long as we could float back down again afterwards."

Reaching the balloon string with our fingers was totally impossible without sitting up on the bed. If our fingers had been about thirty centimetres longer we'd have been able to grab the string easily. Or if the string had been thirty centimetres longer instead.

But it wasn't.

So we sat up and reached it instead.

The **trouble with finally reaching the balloon** is, even when we had hold of the actual balloon there still wasn't very much we could do with it.

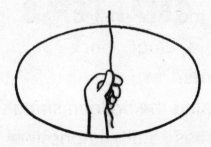

We couldn't play football with it, we couldn't play basketball with it, we couldn't even play "catch" with it, because every time we let go of the balloon it just floated up to the ceiling.

"Shall we have another look at the unicorns?" I said.

"OK," said Gabby.

CHAPTER 8

"Jack Beechwhistle says unicorns are a cross between a horse and a rhinoceros," I said, as Gabby pulled the unicorns out from under her bed.

"Barry Morely doesn't," said Gabby, getting up off her knees and laying the unicorns down on her duvet. "Barry says unicorns are mythical magical beasts."

"What's a mythical magical beast?" I asked.

"It's a make-believe animal that's magical but not real," said Gabby, "like a dragon or a fairy."

104

"A fairy isn't an animal!" I laughed. "Or a beast! Fairies wear dresses!"

"OK, like a dragon or a heffalump," said Gabby. "Which unicorn do you want to look at?"

"The one with the silver hair," I said. "It will match my silver necklace."

"OK," said Gabby, dropping it into my lap. "I'll look at the blue-haired one."

The unicorn with silver hair did look a bit make-believe. Not only did it have silver hair and a sparkly horn, it had fluffy white hooves, a purple smile and stars on its tummy.

Gabby's unicorn looked just as made up too. Not only did it have silver hair and a sparkly horn, it had fluffy blue hooves, a green smile, really long silver eyelashes and rosy red cheeks.

Both unicorns were really soft and cuddly and strokey though.

"There is no way that unicorns are made from bits of rhinoceros," I said. "Rhinoceroses are far too hard and grey and dangerous to be anything to do with unicorns, plus rhinoceros horns aren't in the slightest bit sparkly."

"I think Jack Beechwhistle has more rhinoceros in him than a unicorn does," smiled Gabby.

"I think Jack Beechwhistle is mostly rhinoceros," I chuckled.

"I wonder why it is that unicorns haven't got wings?" said Gabby, holding her unicorn up in the air and then swooping it around like an aeroplane. "I mean, they seem to have everything else. If unicorns had wings they could fly everywhere instead of walk."

"My unicorn doesn't need wings to fly," I giggled. "Look, he uses this balloon!"

Gabby watched me grab the balloon from the ceiling and then clapped her hands as I took my unicorn and the balloon for a pretend ride around her bedroom.

"Look!" I giggled. "I'm not a unicorn, I'm a BALLOONICORN! See!"

Gabby saw all right! She saw so much she nearly fell off the bed laughing.

"A BALLOONICORN called HUGHNICORN!" she laughed, springing to her feet, putting the blue-haired unicorn back on the bed, and then helping me to properly tie the balloon string around my unicorn's tail.

"A BALLOONICORN called HUGHNICORN who's married to a unicorn called PRUNICORN!" I giggled.

Gabby's eyes widened really wide. So did her smile and then so did her arms.

"I'm going to get another balloon!"

she said, giving me a huge hug and then racing back downstairs to grab a balloon from the dining room.

She was back in a flash, which meant in about thirty seconds flat we had one BALLOONICORN called HUGHNICORN and another BALLOONICORN called PRUNICORN to play with!

And we didn't stop there either!

"Let's pretend Hughnicorn and Prunicorn have just got married!" said Gabby.

"Let's pretend they're on their honeymoon!" I said. "Then they'll be…"

"Hughnicorn and Prunicorn the BALLOONICORNHONEYMOONICORNS!!" we both said together!

How hilarious is that!!!

It's a good job Gabby's new house has an upstairs toilet AND a downstairs toilet, because if there had only been one place for us to run to, one of us would definitely have wet ourselves!

"Where shall we fly Hughnicorn and Prunicorn on their honeymoon?" I said, as soon as we got back to Gabby's bedroom.

"My mum and dad's bedroom first," said Gabby, "then the spare room, then the bathroom and then back to the top of the stairs!"

That's the **trouble with BALLOONICORNHONEYMOONICORNS**, they really like to travel!

We flew them over a mountain range made of pillows!

We took them on a funfair ride made
from an exercise bike!

We floated them past a giant waterfall made out of the bath tap!

And when we got to the top of the stairs, we landed to check the knots in our strings.

"Imagine how exciting it would be if we could float them around without holding them in our hands!" I said, putting Hughnicorn down on the carpet at the top of the stairs and letting go of the string.

"You're right," said Gabby, standing Prunicorn next to Hughnicorn and letting go of her string too.

"I wonder how many balloons it would take for them to float up into the air by themselves?" I said.

"LET'S FIND OUT!" said Gabby, grabbing Prunicorn and sliding down the stairs on her bottom.

"WAIT FOR ME!" I giggled,

grabbing Hughnicorn and holding on to the bannister instead.

That's the **trouble with stairs**.

If they're not your stairs you need to be careful. Especially if you've got a Hughnicorn to take care of, too!

CHAPTER 9

Everyone looked really surprised when Gabby and me burst back into the dining room with unicorns tied to birthday balloons.

"WE NEED MORE BALLOONS!" shouted Gabby, jumping up and down all around the table and grabbing as many strings as she could grab. "WE NEED ALL THE BALLOONS!"

"What do you need balloons for?" asked her mum.

"FOR HUGHNICORN AND PRUNICORN TO FLOAT WITH!" explained Gabby.

"Hughnicorn and Prunicorn are the best!"

When Nana Pru heard that we'd called the unicorns Hughnicorn and Prunicorn she got really excited too!

"Hughnicorn AND Prunicorn?!" she gasped. "DID YOU HEAR THAT, HUGH? THEY'VE NAMED THE UNICORNS AFTER US!!!"

Everyone heard it and everyone thought they were brilliant names for our unicorns too!

"Sorry, can't stop!" puffed Gabby, pushing me out of the dining room and racing back up the stairs. "We've got an experiment to do!"

The **trouble with experiments** is sometimes you need to be a scientist to do them.

Gabby and me didn't, though. All Gabby and me needed was Hughnicorn, Prunicorn and loads of helium balloons.

This is how you do a BALLOONICORN experiment at home.

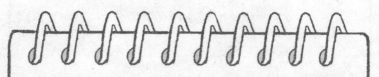

STEP 1: Get the smallest and lightest unicorn you can find.
(Otherwise the experiment

will take ages. And you'll run out of balloons and helium!)

STEP 2: Tie the string of a helium balloon to your unicorn. (Gabby and I had already done that bit; Gabby had chosen PRUNICORN's neck to tie her string to. I had chosen HUGHNICORN's tail.)

STEP 3: Put your unicorn down on the carpet and let the helium balloon float up as high as it will go.

STEP 4: If your unicorn stays on the carpet add another string and balloon.

STEP 5: If your unicorn's feet still stay on the carpet add some more strings and some more balloons.

STEP 6: If your unicorn's feet STILL stay on the carpet add even more strings and even more balloons.

(That's the **trouble with BALLOONICORN** experiments. Unicorns can be a lot heavier than you think.)

STEP 7: Keep tying strings and balloons to your unicorn until its feet actually start to lift off the floor.

(If you tie your strings to your unicorn's neck the front hooves of your unicorn will lift up first. If you tie your strings to your unicorn's tail the back hooves of your unicorn will lift up first.)

STEP 8: Keep tying more strings and balloons to your unicorn until its whole feet lift right off the floor!

STEP 9: Then just keep adding more strings and balloons depending on how high you want them to go!

It took me and Gabby ten balloons each to get our first hooves to lift off the floor.

It took us thirteen balloons each to get Hughnicorn and Prunicorn to lift right up off the carpet.

By sixteen balloons they were floating right up to our T-shirts! All by themselves, on their own, without us even holding them or touching them! IT WAS BRILLIANT!

After we'd done about two thousand fist bumps, Gabby said that Hughnicorn and Prunicorn were the best birthday presents she'd ever had!

"Let's take them outside!" I said. "They can spend the second part of their honeymoon in the garden having the best ballooning adventure EVER!"

Don't worry, I know what you're thinking. We didn't let them fly away!

Once we had managed to squeeze our balloons through the kitchen door, the back door and into Gabby's back garden, there was loads of room to play BALLOONICORNS!

"Fly, Prunicorn, fly!" said Gabby, letting go of Prunicorn and giving her a nudge in the direction of the flowerbeds and the pond.

"Float, Hughnicorn, float!" I said, carrying Hughnicorn into the middle of the lawn to see which way the wind would take him. (If it ever decided to blow.)

"They need to stay together," said Gabby, grabbing Prunicorn and pulling her balloon strings over to where I was standing. "They're on honeymoon together, remember."

Hughnicorn and Prunicorn had an even better honeymoon once they got together in the middle of the lawn.

They floated over an Atlantic Ocean made of fish pond...

some Sahara desert made of sand pit . . .

and even a Great Wall of China made out of flowerpots.

The grown-ups even came out to watch!

"What a clever idea!" said Nana Pru, poking Prunicorn in the side with one of her long blue fingernails and then stepping back to watch her float through the air. "I'm so pleased you love my present!"

"Have you shown Nana and Grandad your new bike?!" shouted Gabby's dad from the back doorstep.

"Can you do it?" Gabby shouted back. "We're flying to New York!"

"Take me with you to Barbados, please!" said Grandad Hugh, forgetting that he wasn't actually a unicorn or a balloonicorn.

After we'd floated Hughnicorn

and Prunicorn past three New York skyscrapers made out of wheelie bins, we decided to let them float wherever they wanted to for a little while. Apart from near the rose beds.

That's the **trouble with rose bushes**. Too many prickles!

"SMILE!!" said Gabby's mum, filming some of Hughnicorn and Prunicorn's balloon adventures on her phone.

Gabby and me couldn't stop smiling!

We smiled from one end of the garden to the other, then back into the house, twice round the lounge, back up the stairs to her bedroom, three times round the front garden and twice round the garage! We even took Hughnicorn and Prunicorn on to the pavement outside Gabby's house and past all of her neighbours' houses too!

"I hope if I get married I go on a honeymoon that's as brilliant fun as this!" said Gabby.

"Me too!" I said. "As long as I fly to Disney World as well."

"Definitely!" said Gabby. "We can go for a fly with Dumbo!"

"That looks like fun, Gabby!" said the lady who lives next door.

"Room for one more?!" said a man who lived on the other side of the road. (He was joking. Our balloons would never have lifted him off the ground. Especially him AND his lawn mower.)

Everyone in Gabby's whole road loved our BALLOONICORNS. Even children who Gabby hadn't met before came over to see what we were doing.

By the time we went back indoors, Hughnicorn and Prunicorn were probably the most famous unicorns in the world. They were definitely the most famous unicorns in Gabby's street.

"I think they're running out of gas!"
frowned Gabby, tugging her balloon
strings upwards and then watching
Prunicorn sink nearer and nearer to the
hallway carpet.

Gabby was definitely right. The helium in our party balloons was definitely going down and down.

"I'll get some scissors and cut the strings," said Gabby, carrying Hughnicorn and Prunicorn back to the kitchen as the doorbell rang and did its amazing three tunes, and her mum answered the front door.

"DAISY! YOUR MUM'S HERE!" she called.

"It can't be seven o'clock already!" I gasped.

But it was! My mum had actually come to collect me ALREADY! Time really does fly when you're flying BALLOONICORNS!

As soon as I saw my mum I ran to tell her that Gabby and me had been playing with our first ever unicorns EVER! PLUS Gabby's nana had BLUE HAIR!

But I didn't get the chance.

"WHERE'S MY SILVER NECKLACE?" gasped my mum the moment she saw me standing in the hallway.

If I was smiling before, I wasn't smiling now. Gabby and me had been playing BALLOONICORNS for so long I'd forgotten all about my silver necklace.

"Only kidding," chuckled Mum. "I'm glad to see you haven't lost it!"

Honestly, when will parents ever learn that there are some things you just don't make jokes about? Like actual solid silver guest of honour necklaces!!!!!!!

CHAPTER 10

"A piece each!" said Gabby's mum, handing my mum two pieces of rainbow birthday cake wrapped up in serviettes.

"Did you make it yourself?" asked my mum, lifting up a corner of the paper to see what flavour cake was inside.

"I decorated it myself," whispered Gabby's mum, inviting my mum into the lounge to meet Nana Pru and Grandad Hugh.

"A unicorn each!" smiled Gabby as soon as our mums were out of sight.

The **trouble with someone saying "a unicorn each"** is no one had ever said "a unicorn each" to me before.

Which meant for a moment I wasn't quite sure if my ears were playing tricks.

"You keep Hughnicorn and I'll keep Prunicorn!" smiled Gabby, pressing Hughnicorn into my hands. "Then every time I come to your house to play or you come to mine, we can each bring our

153

unicorns with us!"

That's right! Cross my heart and hope to die, my ears weren't playing tricks at all!

"But Hughnicorn is one of your birthday presents!" I said, really hoping Gabby wouldn't change her mind.

"I know!" laughed Gabby. "Now he's your *Guest of Honour* present instead!"

The **trouble with being given a guest of honour present** is that had never happened to me before either!

"But what will your mum and dad say?" I gulped, still a bit worried that Gabby might get into trouble for giving one of her presents away to me.

"I've already asked them," said Gabby. "They think it's a brilliant idea!"

"But what about your nana and grandad?" I asked.

"I've already asked them too!" she laughed. "They like you almost as much as I do!"

It was true! Can you believe it? I was actually, actually, actually going to be going home from Gabby's birthday party with an actual present of my own!

And a piece of cake!!

"They can be best friends just like us!" I said. "Why don't you bring Prunicorn round to my house tomorrow and we can play unicorns all day!"

"I will!" laughed Gabby as my mum came back from the lounge wiping cake crumbs from her mouth.

That's the **trouble with slices of rainbow birthday cake**.

Mums can't resist them!

I couldn't resist Gabby's doorbell either!!

"SEE YOU TOMORROW MORNING!" I shouted.

CHAPTER 11

"Look what Gabby's given me!" I said, skipping down the path with Hughnicorn under my arm. "He's coming home with us to live with me in my bedroom!"

"I know, Daisy," said my mum. "Aren't you lucky!"

"Guess what else!" I said, as we walked to our car. "Gabby's Nana Pru has got BLUE HAIR!"

"I know that too, Daisy," Mum said. "I've just been talking to her in the lounge!"

"You noticed it then!" I said.

159

"Of course I noticed it," she sighed. "It wasn't hard to miss."

"Why do you think she's turned her hair blue?" I asked, doing up Hughnicorn's seat belt first and then fastening mine up second.

"Because she's a lady of a certain age," said my mum.

"What's a lady of a certain age?" I asked, blowing Gabby a kiss as we drove away.

"It's a lady in her later years who decides she wants to add a little something extra to the way she looks," said my mum.

"To make her look bluer?" I said.

"To make her look younger," Mum said.

"When are you going to do that?" I asked.

"I'm not going to do it," said Mum, "and before you tell me all the reasons I should do it, just remember it's a very long walk home!"

When we got back to my house I couldn't wait to go to bed. Neither could Hughnicorn. We'd been whispering to each other all the way home without my mum being able to hear. That's right, all the way home in the car, in actual human language, all the way up my garden path and all the way into my house!

How magical is that!

As soon as we got indoors my mum said that before I did anything I needed to put Hughnicorn down, take her silver necklace off and put it safely back on the dressing table in her bedroom. She said that she was really, really pleased that I hadn't broken it. So pleased in fact, she was going to read me an extra bedtime story that night!

Except I didn't want Mum to read me a bedtime story that night. I just wanted to talk to Hughnicorn.

"I'm too tired for bedtime stories, thanks Mum," I fibbed. "Being guest of honour at Gabby's party has really worn me out!"

Mum was so surprised to hear how tired I was, she put her hand on my forehead to see if I had a temperature.

"Do you feel all right?"

"Yes," I said.

"But you can't be all right."

"Why can't I be all right?" I asked.

"Because you never want to go to bed."

"I do tonight," I said. "So does my unicorn."

"Are you sure you haven't done something to my silver necklace?" she frowned.

"Positive," I said, undoing it right in front of her and putting it into her hands.

"And you're positive you don't want me to read you two bedtime stories instead of one?" she said, looking at every single bit of silver necklace really closely.

"Yes," I said.

"Or even one bedtime story?" she said.

"Yes," I said, "I don't want you to read me any bedtime stories tonight at all, thank you."

"You just want to go to bed?" she said.

"Yes," I said.

"By yourself?"

"With my unicorn," I said.

"And you don't mind putting your pyjamas on by yourself?"

"No, I don't mind putting my pyjamas

on by myself," I said.

"And you don't mind washing your face and hands by yourself?"

"That's right," I said.

"And you will clean your teeth as well?" she said.

"I will clean my teeth as well." I nodded.

"Up and down and all around and not just side to side?"

"Up and down and all around and not just side to side."

"Without me having to watch?"

"Without you having to watch."

And I did!

Well, me and Hughnicorn did.

"I'll get you a drink of water," said Mum as she tucked me into bed.

"I don't need a drink of water tonight, thanks," I said.

"But you always have a drink of water when you go to bed." Mum frowned.

"I don't need one tonight, thanks," I said.

"Can I still give you a goodnight kiss?" she asked.

"Of course you can!" I said, leaning forward and giving my mum a big kiss. "And then can you close my bedroom door when you go, please?"

"Pardon?" Mum gulped, standing in the doorway of my bedroom and

looking a bit stiff.

"Can you close the door of my bedroom when you go, please?" I asked.

"But you always sleep with your bedroom door open!" said my mum.

"Not tonight," I said, snuggling Hughnicorn into my pillow.

"Are you absolutely sure you're feeling all right, Daisy?" said my mum.

"I'm absolutely sure," I smiled.

"And you're sure you have got everything you need?" she asked.

"I'm absolutely sure I have everything I need," I said, stroking Hughnicorn's hair with my finger.

My mum ran out of words after that.

CHAPTER 12

When I woke up the next morning I was absolutely bursting with things to tell Gabby about unicorns, things that even Barry Morely wouldn't have known! Things that the whole wide actual world wouldn't have known! Because guess what, without my mum even knowing I had been talking to HUGHNICORN ALL NIGHT! Well until my mum came back into my bedroom and took my three-colour torch off me, and that was midnight at least!

Even in the dark, Hughnicorn and

me had kept on whispering. We talked about all the things unicorns did, all the places unicorns went, the things unicorns liked – Hughnicorn told me stories about unicorns that no one even knows existed!

Wait till you hear this!

Unicorns who wore shoes were called SHOENICORNS!

Unicorns who were blue were called BLUENICORNS!

And unicorns who told the truth were called TRUENICORNS!

Hughnicorn was definitely telling the truth, which made him a

BALLOONICORNHONEYMOONICORN-
BLUENICORNTRUENICORN!

If he'd had shoes on his feet instead of hooves he would have been a BALLOONICORN HONEYMOONICORNBLUENICORN-TRUENICORNSHOENICORN!

How magical would THAT have been!!!

I was absolutely desperate to tell Gabby all of my unicorn news! In fact I rang her up and told her not to even bother having breakfast and get round to my house straight away. Oh and not to forget to bring Prunicorn either!

Gabby was absolutely desperate to see me too! She still didn't arrive until ten past ten though, because her dad had made her try out her new bike before she came to play.

That's the **trouble with new bikes**, sometimes they can really get in the way of having fun.

It didn't matter though, because guess what! Gabby had spent all night under the covers talking to Prunicorn too! And double guess what?? Prunicorn had told her things about unicorns that Hughnicorn hadn't even told me!

Did you know a unicorn that wakes you up in the morning is called a COCKADOODLEDOONICORN!

Did you know a unicorn with a red bottom is called a BABOONICORN?

And did you know that a unicorn who is very polite is called a HOWDOYOUDONICORN?

I didn't. BUT I DID NOW!

As soon as Gabby told me about COCKADOODLEDOONICORNS I fell on to my bed and started laughing all over the place. I was laughing so much I could hardly breathe! I was still on my back when she said HOWDOYOUDONICORN!

It was the start of something **MASSIVE**!

"Let's ask Hughnicorn and Prunicorn loads more questions about unicorns!" I said, picking Hughnicorn up and pressing my lips to his ear. "Let's find out every single thing about unicorns that there is to know!"

"We could write a book!" squealed Gabby. "We could call it the WHO'SWHONICORN OF UNICORNS!" she squealed.

There was no stopping us after that. Well, there wasn't once we had finally managed to stop giggling and start breathing again!

For the next five days of the summer holiday Gabby and I met up in each other's bedrooms and found out everything about unicorns there is to know. Starting with the very first unicorn ever invented!

Here it is then! THE WHO's-WHONICORN OF UNICORNS by DAISY BUTTERS AND GABRIELLA SUMMERS!!!!!!! (With a lot of help from Hughnicorn and Prunicorn!)

I HOPE YOU LIKE OUR BOOK!

THE WHO'SWHONICORN OF UNICORNS!

By Daisy Butters
and
Gabriella Summers

IN THE BEGINNING there was only one single unicorn in the whole wide universe.

He was called NEWNICORN because he was very new. He was also very lonely.

So TWONICORNS were invented as well.
TWONICORNS went everywhere in twos...

until FEWNICORNS were invented too.

Before long there were unicorns of all shapes and sizes!

Baby unicorns were called GAGGAGOONICORNS.

BLUENICORNS were blue.

MAROONICORNS were maroon.

ANYCOLOURYOULIKEIT'SUPTOYOUNI-
CORNS were any colour or colours they
wanted to be.

All unicorns loved having their hair done.

The ones that did the hair-washing were called
SHAMPOONICORNS.

The ones who did the hair-cutting were called
HAIRDONICORNS.

CANOENICORNS lived on the river. They
went everywhere by canoe.

Living on the river was really
good fun unless there was a
HARPOONICORN hiding in
the reeds, trying to get you.

BALLOONICORNS
had to watch out for
HARPOONICORNS too.

LOONICORNS lived down the loo.

Smelly LOONICORNS were called
POONICORNS.

Extremely smelly ones were called
STINKYPOONICORNS.

Most unicorns weren't smelly at all.

The scariest unicorns were called BOO!NICORNS. BOO!NICORNS hid behind trees and lampposts and jumped out on other unicorns all the time.

MOONICORNS only came out at night.

MOONICORNS who came out when there was a full moon were called FULLMOONICORNS.

The clumsiest unicorns were called BUMPINTONICORNS. BUMPINTONICORNS bumped into things everywhere they went. They were always covered in plasters and bruises.

CUCKOONICORNS lived in trees and went "Cuckoo!" all day. And all night.

LOOPYLOONICORNS were a bit bonkers. Their horn was on their bottom instead of on their head.

Invisible unicorns were called SEETHROUGHNICORNS. Sometimes SEETHROUGHNICORNS would creep up on BOO!NICORNS and make them jump instead!

The happiest unicorns were called YAHOONICORNS.

The UNhappiest were called BOOHOONICORNS.

Their best friends were TISSUENICORNS.

The best unicorn fighters were called
KUNGFUNICORNS. KUNGFUNICORNS were
black belts in everything!

PUNYCORNS were really weedy.

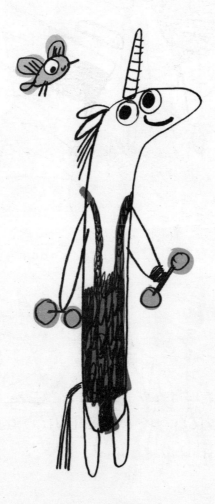

GLUENICORNS stuck together.

SUPERGLUENICORNS stuck together even more.

Unicorns who ate really hot curry were called VINDALOONICORNS.

Unicorns who preferred stew were called STEWNICORNS.

There were three types of STEWNICORN; CHICKENSTEWNICORNS, BEEFSTEWNICORNS and LAMBSTEWNICORNS.

HOWDOYOUDONICORNS
were very polite.

THANKYOUNICORNS
were very grateful.

AFTERYOUNICORNS
had really good manners.

NO, AFTERYOUNICORNS
had even better manners.

QUEUENICORNS loved standing in long lines.

SNOOKERCUENICORNS were really good at snooker.

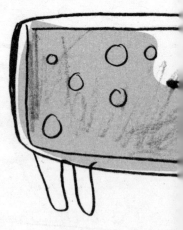

POOLCUENICORNS were really good
at pool.

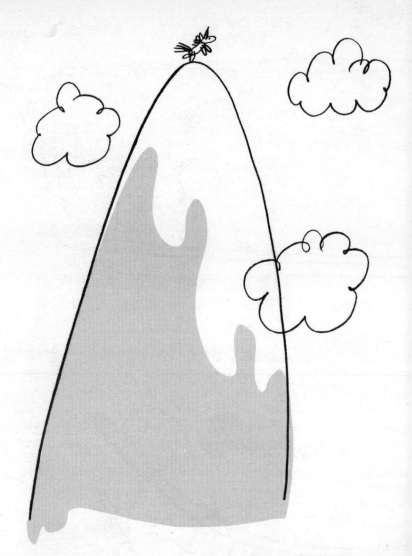

Unicorns who lived on the top of really high mountains were called LOOKATTHATVIEW!NICORNS.

NOTHINGTODONICORNS got bored really easily.

Really noisy unicorns were called HULLABALLOONICORNS.

GREWNICORNS never stopped growing.
They just grew and grew and grew.

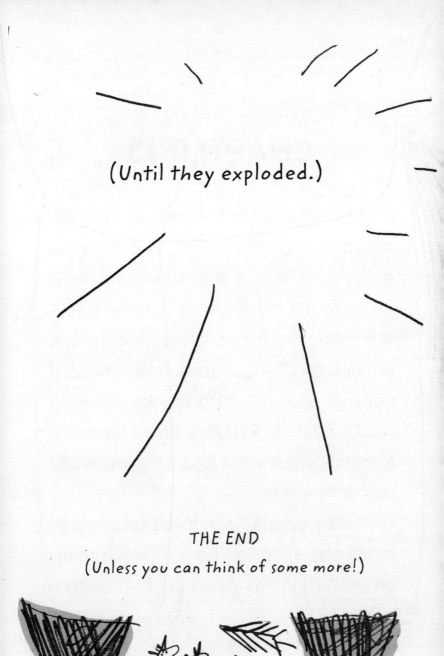

(Until they exploded.)

THE END
(Unless you can think of some more!)

CHAPTER 13

If you'd told me at the beginning of the
school holiday that Gabby and me were
going to be able to write a book all about
unicorns I'd never have believed you!
But suddenly, thanks to Hughnicorn and
Prunicorn, we had gone from knowing
nothing about unicorns to knowing
ABSOLUTELY EVERYTHING about unicorns!
Me and Gabby were total absolute world
unicorn experts!!!

Gabby decided she loved unicorns so
much she spent all her birthday money
on unicorn things. She bought a unicorn

duvet for her bed and unicorn covers for her pillows. She chose unicorn wallpaper for her bedroom and a unicorn lampshade for her bedside light. She even bought a unicorn hot water bottle to warm her toes up with. IN THE MIDDLE OF THE SUMMER!

Gabby's bedroom looked amazing!

I didn't have any birthday money to spend on my bedroom because it wasn't my birthday, so my bedroom ended up looking pretty much the same. Apart from when Hughnicorn was in it.

I did ask my mum if I could have next year's birthday money early, but she said no. I even asked her if we could have Christmas early this year instead. But she still said no.

So I decided to dye my hair unicorn colours instead.

The **trouble with dying your hair unicorn colours** is it should really be totally up to you, because it's your hair, not your mum's. Especially if you really, really want to do it.

When I saw Gabby yesterday and told her that I had decided to dye my hair unicorn colours she thought it was a brilliant idea!

"What colour are you going to go for?" asked Gabby.

"Sparkly red," I said, "with maybe some pinky-purple."

"Where will you get the colours from?" she asked.

"I'll have a look in the bathroom," I said, changing my mind again to sparkly red and shimmery orange. Or maybe just shimmery orange.

That's the **trouble with unicorn colours**. There are so many to choose from.

"Have you told your mum you're going to dye your hair?" she said.

"She's sunbathing," I said, "she won't want me to disturb her. And in any case, my mum dyes her hair all the time."

"REALLY?" gasped Gabby.

"REALLY!" I nodded. "She'd look about a hundred if she didn't."

Gabby and me grabbed Hughnicorn and Prunicorn from my bed and raced to the bathroom to see what colour hair dye we could find.

"SEE!" I said, taking a packet out of the bathroom cabinet. "Actual hair dye!"

"It doesn't look very unicorny," said Gabby, frowning at the colour on the packet.

Gabby was right. My mum's hair dye was called "URBAN TEMPTRESS" and it was the colour of a sucked toffee.

The **trouble with sucked toffee** is no unicorn wants their hair to look like sucked toffee. Sucked toffees aren't in the slightest bit magical at all.

So we had to think of another way of doing the colour.

"What about colouring pens?" said Gabby.

"Mine are mostly running out," I said.

"The ones in my pencil case are too," said Gabby.

That's the **trouble with colouring pens**. They don't put enough colour inside the pens.

"Has *your* mum got any hair dye I can borrow?" I asked.

"I don't think so," said Gabby. "She always gets her hair done at the hairdressers. The only thing in our bathroom cabinet that has colour in it is toothpaste."

"That's a shame," I said. "I can't colour my hair with toothpaste, unless we can get the blue bit out of the stripes."

"What about food colouring!" Gabby said. "My mum has got loads of different food colourings in her kitchen drawer. She used them to colour the rainbow on my birthday cake!"

As soon as Gabby said "food colouring" I knew we were really on to something!

"My mum's got food colourings too!" I said. "Well, she's definitely got green and red because we used them to do our Christmas cake last Christmas!"

"My mum's got loads of colours," said Gabby. "Not just rainbow colours either!"

"Has she got shimmery orange?" I asked.

"She's definitely got orange!" she said. "I'm not sure how shimmery it is."

"What about sparkly red?" I asked. "I'd really like my hair to sparkle!"

"She might have," said Gabby. "I won't know until I get home and look in my kitchen drawer."

"OK! Then that's what we'll do," I said. "We'll spend the rest of the day playing with Hughnicorn and Prunicorn and then when your mum takes you home later, we can both get as many different colourings out of our kitchen drawers as we can!"

"Without our mums seeing," said Gabby.

"DEFINITELY without our mums seeing."
I nodded.

"Otherwise it won't be a surprise!" said Gabby.

"ABSOLUTELY." I nodded again. "I absolutely definitely want it to be a surprise!"

CHAPTER 14

When Gabby came to call for me this morning she had a smile as wide as a banana. She'd found so many food colourings in her mum's kitchen drawer she'd had to carry them round in her school bag. (Without her mum knowing, of course.)

"Where's your mum?" she whispered as we went upstairs to my bedroom.

"Sunbathing," I said.

"Already?!" said Gabby. "It's only half past nine!"

"She loves sunbathing," I told her.

"She won't come up and see us, will she?" said Gabby.

"Not if the sun's shining," I told her.

As soon as we got into my bedroom Gabby tipped her food colourings on to my bed. When I saw how many she had brought I nearly fainted! She had Sky Blue, Navy Blue, Royal Blue. There was Bright Pink, Deep Pink, Rose Pink. She had Lemon Yellow, Golden Yellow, Satsuma Orange, Sunset Orange, Melba Peach. There was Tulip Red, Cherry Red, Super Red. There was Violet. There was Mint Green. There was Turquoise. There was even Black!

"How many colours were *you* able to

get?" Gabby asked.

"Holly Berry Red and Holly Leaf Green," I said. Which was good actually, because Gabby hadn't brought either of those.

The **trouble with having so many colours to choose from** is it was impossible to choose.

So I chose them all.

"ALL OF THEM?!" gasped Gabby.

"Yes," I said. "Colour my hair like a rainbow! I bet unicorns absolutely love rainbows!"

Gabby agreed one hundred per cent. Well, ninety-nine.

"Maybe not black," she said. "I'm not sure rainbows have black in them."

"In that case, put all the other colours on my hair first," I said, "and then we can decide whether to add the black as well afterwards."

"Are you sure your mum won't come up and see us?" Gabby asked.

"There isn't a cloud in the sky," I said, looking out of my bedroom window to make sure my mum was still lying on her back. "Start colouring!"

The **trouble with colouring hair like a rainbow** is it takes a bit of practice at first. Especially if you've never coloured someone's hair with food colouring before. Doubly especially if you haven't brought anything to actually put the colours on with either.

The **trouble with pouring the colours on** is sometimes too much comes out of the bottle all at once. Which means the colouring doesn't just go on your hair, it runs down your hair and on to the shoulders of your T-shirt too.

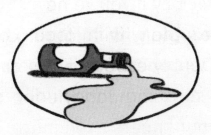

So Gabby tried dabbing the colour on with her fingers instead.

The **trouble with dabbing colour on with your fingers** is it didn't just put colour on to my hair, it put colour on to Gabby's fingers too.

So Gabby tried wrapping her fingers in loo roll first, to see if that made it easier.

The **trouble with colouring hair with fingers wrapped up in loo roll** is the colours soak through the loo roll and colour your fingers even more.

"I hope the colours come out," said Gabby, sucking her fingers.

"You've got the colours on your lips now," I said.

"Oops!" she said, wiping her lips with the back of her hand.

"Now you've got the colours on the back of your hand!" I laughed.

Thank goodness I found a paint brush in my craft drawer!

Once I'd found a paint brush small enough for Gabby to use, we were in business! All Gabby had to do was dip the brush in the colouring bottles and paint the rainbow stripes on my hair!

"Here I go!" said Gabby, doing her first dip and then painting the first stripe.

"Try not to move," she said, "I don't want the rainbow to be wobbly."

"How's it looking?" I asked, after she'd done some of the reds, blues and yellows.

"REALLY GOOD!" said Gabby.

"How's it looking now?" I said after she'd done some of the oranges, pinks and greens.

"I think some of the stripes need to dry a bit," said Gabby, "but I'm sure when they do, they'll look even better than a rainbow!"

"If you were a unicorn and you saw my hair, would you be jealous?" I asked.

"DEFINITELY," said Gabby.

"Do you think Hughnicorn looks jealous?" I smiled.

"Deffo!" said Gabby.

"Do you think Prunicorn looks jealous?"

"Double deffo!!" laughed Gabby.

"I can't wait to see what I look like." I grinned.

"I can't wait to show you!" smiled Gabby.

I don't know how many colourings we had for our rainbow stripes but it took absolutely ages to paint them all on.

"TA DAH!" said Gabby, finally leading me into the bathroom, standing me in front of the bathroom mirror and then telling me to open my eyes.

"Which colour is which?" I asked, opening my eyes but expecting to see a bit more of a rainbow than I was seeing.

"I can't exactly remember. I think this browny-reddish stripe is the Cherry Red." She pointed. "This browny-yellowish stripe is the Golden Yellow, this browny-greenish stripe is Mint Green, and this browny-pinkish stripe is definitely Deep Pink."

"I thought you weren't going to use black?" I said, pointing to the darkest stripe of all.

"That's the Royal Blue," said Gabby.

"It's a bit more browny than I was hoping," I said, starting to wonder whether Gabby was as good at doing rainbows as she said.

"Don't forget your hair is quite brown in the first place," said Gabby, "and don't forget the colours haven't dried properly yet. When you get out into the sunshine I'm sure the stripes will look just like a rainbow."

"Will they sparkle too?" I asked. "I'd REALLY like them to sparkle."

"You bet they will, I'm going to make sure of it!" she said, grabbing me by the hand and tugging me back into the bedroom. "Wait till you see my special sparkly ingredient!" she said, sitting me back on my bed and then unzipping the front pocket of her school bag. "If this doesn't make your rainbow colours sparkle, nothing will!"

The **trouble with glitter glue** is it doesn't just have glitter in it, it has glue in it too. So when Gabby started painting glitter glue stripes on to my hair, things got a little bit sticky.

"I think that's enough sparkle," said Gabby, when the paint brush started sticking to my ear. "Let's go and show your mum!"

CHAPTER 15

"SURPRISE!" we shouted, stepping out into the garden to show Mum my new rainbow hair!

The **trouble with waking up my mum when she's sunbathing is** I think she got cross before she even had the time to get surprised.

She was definitely *more* cross than surprised. Definitely, definitely, definitely, definitely.

"OH MY GOOD GIDDY AUNT, WHAT ON EARTH HAVE YOU DONE TO YOUR HAIR, DAISY?" she gasped.

"Coloured it!" I said.

"And sparkled it!" said Gabby.

"Like a rainbow!" I said, just in case she hadn't worked that bit out.

I can't tell you what my mum said after that. Your ears would fall off I did. And your eyeballs would fall out. And your eyebrows would fall off.

She definitely wasn't very happy with my new rainbow hair though. AT ALL.

I can tell you she rang Gabby's mum straight away and asked her to take Gabby home. Then she made me get straight in the bath and wash my hair about a hundred times. In the middle of the actual day!

"What were you thinking!" she said, tipping another whole bottle of shampoo on my head and then rubbing my hair really hard. "Thank goodness you don't have to go to school for the next five weeks!"

"I wanted to colour my hair like a unicorn, that's all," I said.

"Children do not colour their own hair!" said my mum. "Especially like a unicorn!"

"You colour your own hair!" I said.

"Not like a unicorn I don't!" she said.

"Gabby's Nana Pru does!" I said. "Gabby's Nana Pru colours her hair ACTUAL BLUE! SHE looks like a unicorn.

She said so herself!"

My mum still stayed cross though.

"I told you before, Daisy, Gabby's Nana Pru is a lady of a certain age! That's what ladies of a certain age do!" she said.

"Well, I'm a girl of a certain age and I am certain I want my hair to be rainbow coloured!"

But Mum still wouldn't listen.

She rubbed my hair and she scrubbed my hair and she pulled glue from my hair and then she started all over again!

And then . . . can you believe it . . .

SHE CONFISCATED MY UNICORN!

So Hughnicorn is living in my loft at the moment, really high up out of reach.

Prunicorn is living really high up in Gabby's loft at the moment too.

They didn't use helium balloons to float themselves up there either.

I don't think I'll be seeing Hughnicorn for a while now.

SIGH.

I don't think Gabby will be seeing Prunicorn for a while either.

I really, really, really wish Gabby and Hughnicorn and Prunicorn were here with me now.

TRIPLE SIGH.

They'd absolutely LOVE our new rainbow-coloured bath!

Dear ~~Ostrich Penguin~~ Puffin,

Me and my best friend Gabby have written the best unicorn story EVER in the WHOLE WIDE WORLD! Please will you ask Kes Gray and Garry Parsons to turn it into an actual, actual book with real colour pictures and a shiny cover?

And pages, don't forget the pages.

We can't afford to pay them anything but we promise we will let them both put their names on the cover.

(Really small.)

Yours ~~sinseerly sinserely~~ sincerely

Daisy Butters and ~~Gabriella~~ Gabby Summers.

P.S. If Kes and Garry don't know what a unicorn is, show them the unicorn picture on this note paper.

P.P.S. Gabby bought it with some of her birthday money.

PUFFIN BOOKS

Dear Daisy and Gabby,

Thank you for your letter and your wonderful unicorn story.

We have spoken to Garry and Kes and they would be delighted to help you turn it into an actual, actual book with a shiny cover, colour pictures and pages.

They think the unicorns in your story are very funny and have even started to think of other unicorns of their own!

Apparently, they have started work on the cover already and just have one question. It's about the size of their names.

How small is small?

Yours sincerely,

Puffin

Dear Puffin,

About the size of an ant.

Yours sincerely
Daisy and Gabby.

P.S. When will our book be ready?

PUFFIN BOOKS

Dear Daisy and Gabby,

In about a year's time.

Yours sincerely,

Puffin

A YEAR'S TIME!!!!!!

We can't wait THAT LONG!

A YEAR'S TIME IS AGES!!!!!!!!

PUFFIN BOOKS

Dear Daisy and Gabby,

We're very sorry, but actual, actual books really do take a long time to make.

Garry will have to draw AND colour in all of the pictures.

Kes will have to check all of the spellings. AND all of the full stops and commas.

The cover will need to be designed AND shined.

Plus there will be lots of other design things to be done too.

And printing things.

And shipping things.

That's the trouble with children's books. The best ones take ages and ages to make.

Yours gratefully,

Puffin

P.S. We promise you it will be worth waiting for!

Dear Puffin,

OK.

Yours sincerely
SIGH.

P.S. DOUBLE SIGH.

DAISY'S
TROUBLE INDEX

The trouble with . . .